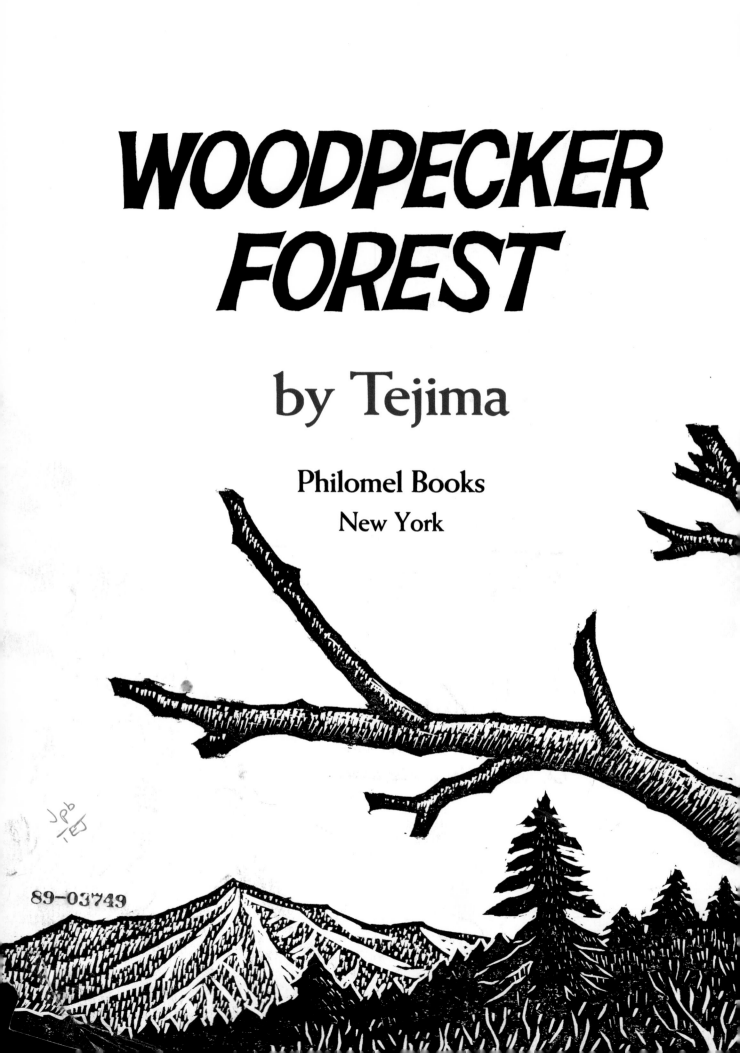

WOODPECKER FOREST

by Tejima

Philomel Books

New York

In the middle of a faraway forest it is almost spring.

The warm wind carries the sound of pecking
through the trees.

Up in a tall tree, a mother and father woodpecker take turns making a hole for their nest. This is where they will raise their family.

When the forest turns a deep green, three baby
woodpeckers are born in the tall tree.

The mother and father woodpecker are busy looking
for food all day long.

They find ants and other insects in old stumps.

The forest echoes with the sounds of their pecking
and the voices of the young birds.

Soon the chirping of cicadas begins.

The baby woodpeckers grow bigger every day.

The time comes
for the young
woodpeckers to try their
wings. With his parents calling,
the bravest of the three flies out of the nest.

The young bird clings to a big tree
and waits for his father to feed him.
All day he clings to the tree.

When the moon rises and the owls begin to hoot,
the bravest young woodpecker is afraid.

A hollow tree full of woodpecker
holes seems to stare at him.

A strange sound fills the forest.

It is as if all the woodpecker trees in the forest are laughing. The shadows of the trees sway in the moonlight.

The young woodpecker calls out for his parents.
Then he hears the sound of wild pecking close by.

He thinks he sees his father,
huge against the sky.
All the trees are silent.

At daybreak, his father appears out of the mist.

The young bird's
wings grow
stronger. He learns
from his parents
how to hunt for
food, and not to
be frightened of
hollow trees.

When snow falls on the mountains, it is time for the
young woodpecker to live on his own.

In the middle of a
cold winter night,
he awakens and
sees the forest
glittering under
the full moon.

A dead tree covered with snow seems to stare at him,
but he isn't afraid. He remembers the first night away
from the nest.

And remembers the way his father filled the whole night sky.

Over the woodpeckers' forest the stars are shining.

From far away comes the hoot of an owl.

American text copyright © 1989 by Philomel Books. Text and
illustrations copyright © 1984 Keizaburō Tejima. All rights re-
served. Published in the United States by Philomel Books, a
division of The Putnam & Grosset Group, 200 Madison Avenue,
New York, NY 10016. Published simultaneously in Canada.
Originally published under the title *Kumagera no mori* by
Fukutake Pub. Co., Ltd., 2-3-28 Kudanminami, Chiyoda-ku,
Tokyo, Japan. Based on an English translation by Susan Matsui.
Printed in Hong Kong by South China Printing Company. Book
Design by Christy Hale.

Library of Congress Cataloging-in-Publication Data Tejima,
Keizaburō. [Kumagera no mori. English] Woodpecker forest /
written and illustrated by Tejima [Keizaburō]. p. cm. Translation
of: Kumagera no mori. Summary: Follows the activities of a
woodpecker family living in the forest from the making of the
nest and hatching of their young through the youngsters' growth
and maturity. 1. Woodpeckers—Juvenile fiction. [1. Woodpeckers—Fiction. 2. Birds—Fiction.] I. Title. PZ10.3.T22Wo
1989 [E]—dc19 88-17888 CIP AC ISBN 0-399-21618-9
First Impression